Poor Behavior

Theresa Rebeck

A Samuel French Acting Edition

SAMUEL FRENCH

FOUNDED 1830

SAMUELFRENCH.COM
SAMUELFRENCH-LONDON.CO.UK

FOR PRODUCTION ENQUIRIES

UNITED STATES AND CANADA
Info@SamuelFrench.com
1-866-598-8449

UNITED KINGDOM AND EUROPE
Plays@SamuelFrench-London.co.uk
020-7255-4302

Each title is subject to availability from Samuel French, depending upon
country of performance. Please be aware that *POOR BEHAVIOR* may
not be licensed by Samuel French in your territory. Professional and
amateur producers should contact the nearest Samuel French office or
licensing partner to verify availability.

MUSIC USE NOTE

Licensees are solely responsible for obtaining formal written permission from copyright owners to use copyrighted music in the performance of this play and are strongly cautioned to do so. If no such permission is obtained by the licensee, then the licensee must use only original music that the licensee owns and controls. Licensees are solely responsible and liable for all music clearances and shall indemnify the copyright owners of the play(s) and their licensing agent, Samuel French, against any costs, expenses, losses and liabilities arising from the use of music by licensees. Please contact the appropriate music licensing authority in your territory for the rights to any incidental music.

IMPORTANT BILLING AND CREDIT REQUIREMENTS

If you have obtained performance rights to this title, please refer to your licensing agreement for important billing and credit requirements.

POOR BEHAVIOR had its world premiere produced by Primary Stages at The Duke on 42nd Street in New York City on July 29, 2014. The production was directed by Evan Cabnet, with sets by Lauren Helpern, costumes by Jessica Pabst, lighting by Jason Lyons, and sound by Jill BC Du Boff. The Production Stage Manager was Samantha Greene. The cast was as follows:

PETER	Jeff Biehl
MAUREEN	Heidi Armbruster
ELLA	Katie Kreisler
IAN	Brian Avers

Poor Behavior was developed at Perry-Mansfield New Works Festival in Steamboat Springs, Colorado.

Poor Behavior was originally produced by Center Theater Group/Mark Taper Forum, Michael Ritchie, Artistic Director; Los Angeles, California, in September 2011.

CHARACTERS

PETER – self-assured, funny, confident, very likeable; a caretaker.

MAUREEN – high-strung, narcissistic, often hysterical;
has a ready self-pity.

ELLA – good-natured, passionate, idealistic, with just enough self-deception at her disposal.

IAN – Irish; has lived in the states for over ten years; bitter, funny, brilliant; he is angry at himself for all his bad decisions. Angry at the universe, too. Ready to burn the store to get what he wants. Is also wounded and vulnerable; it's important that his woundedness be seen.

SETTING

A comfortable weekend home in the country

TIME

Present

ACT ONE

(A large kitchen in a comfortably lavish country home. The remains of dinner on the table. ELLA is pouring the ends of a bottle of wine. IAN is making half an attempt to clear plates while he argues with her. MAUREEN and PETER sit at the table and try to get a word in edgewise. IAN is Irish; the rest, Americans. All are talking on top of each other.)

IAN. You've got to be kidding me. / You really have just got to –

ELLA. *(laughing)* Oh my god the sneering has already begun and I didn't even say anything –

IAN. Sneering? I'm clearing the table. / I'm gathering dinnerware! –

ELLA. You're revving yourself up to sneer and condescend – I can see it coming a mile off.

IAN. I'm Irish, we never condescend. Or sneer. / An Irishman, sneering, no, we twinkle –

ELLA. You spiritually condescend. You literarily condescend / twinkle?

IAN. I'm not doing anything except clearing the table.

MAUREEN. You're mostly just standing around and waving utensils –

IAN. Can the forks wait for fifteen seconds while I deal with this bizarre accusation / that somehow I am about to undermine our hostess's adorable observation.

ELLA. It's not an accusation, oh my god – adorable?

IAN. *(overriding)* CAN I GET TO MY POINT?

PETER. I'm sort of hoping you won't.

ELLA. Well, then what is goodness? What does the word even mean?

IAN. It's a judgmental fantasy –

ELLA. A what?

IAN. – concocted by the religious right to justify an increasingly narrow political agenda –

ELLA. *(ignoring this)* So if I say, "this wine is good –"

IAN. If you said that I'd have to say you're insane –

MAUREEN. I like it!

ELLA. All right then the ice cream is good –

PETER. Is there ice cream? I'd love some ice cream. Anybody else want ice cream?

MAUREEN. I think the wine is good.

PETER. I think the wine's pretty good too.

IAN. It's crap.

MAUREEN. We paid twenty two dollars a bottle, it's from Hungary, this is the new good stuff, I heard it on NPR.

ELLA. I don't care what is good –

IAN. Then what are we arguing about?

PETER. My point exactly.

ELLA. I mean I'm not interested in good in a relative sense, someone will say this is good or that is good –

IAN. Because the word means nothing –

ELLA. No that's my point it doesn't mean nothing –

IAN. But what does it mean, that you can't say.

ELLA. It's a very simple concept, goodness –

IAN. Lord god save us from American idealism –

ELLA. No you're not allowed to reduce –

PETER. And you're not allowed to mention god, god is off the table –

IAN. I'm not convinced he's good anyway –

ELLA. More than half the world believes in god –

PETER. god is off the table!

ELLA. OK but some things are just good. Trees are good.

IAN. Not all trees.

ELLA. Yes. All trees are good.

IAN. If a tree falls on your house, that's not a good tree.

ELLA. It didn't plan to fall on your house, it didn't do it maliciously –

IAN. Is there more of this bad wine?

PETER. Didn't we decide it's good?

ELLA. If the wine can't be good, it can't be bad either.

PETER. I want more bad wine too.

ELLA. I'm tired of everyone making fun of this. Any hope that that there is such a thing, somewhere, as goodness –

PETER. Or "simple human decency," who said that –

ELLA. Mr. Smith, that's Mr. Smith –

IAN. You would know that –

ELLA. Yes that makes me a stupid American well I'm not stupid and I'm not ashamed of knowing that, why do you think that's something I should be embarrassed about?

IAN. It's not quite the same thing as "their eyes mid many wrinkles, their eyes, their ancient glittering eyes are gay" – that's Mr. Yates to the lot of you.

PETER. You guys –

ELLA. Sneering, it's the worst kind of unsophisticated childish, self-centered nasty –

PETER. El, come on.

ELLA. I'm sick of all this European superiority; the Irish haven't done anything except get drunk and write poems for a thousand years.

MAUREEN. Come on, Ella –

IAN. No, it's fine, I might actually concede that point – the poems are good, though, we maybe should get some credit for that –

ELLA. *(overlap, loud)* No the poems can't be good because there's no such thing as goodness according to you.

IAN. All right then they're –

ELLA. No. No. You mourn beautifully and everything's "Jaysus fecking oh and so and there y'are Mrs. Mahoney oh Jaysus wept –"

PETER. Ella!

ELLA. And and and all that bitter Catholic judgement when, okay, you're just mad that America has all the money.

PETER. I just think this is getting a little –

IAN. You're the one who got all hung up on goodness.

ELLA. That's it, isn't it. I believe in goodness so I'm a crazy American.

PETER. No one said that!

ELLA. Yes he did, he said –

IAN. I didn't say it but if you like, I will: You believe in goodness while meanwhile by the way your country gobbles up global resources, pollutes the planet, and that's not even mentioning the the criminals you've put in charge of your banking system stealing all the money from the poor and tap dancing all the way back to their friends on Capitol Hill.

ELLA. *(overlap)* Okay if you're going to bring in –

IAN. *(overlap)* And yet you still coo about this idea of American exceptionalism /so yes that makes you a CRAZY FUCKING AMERICAN.

ELLA. *(overlap)* I am not defending American exceptionalism you know very well I find all of that ridiculous and you are distorting what I'm saying –

IAN. I don't know that – it IS what you're saying –

PETER. *(overlap)* ELLA.

MAUREEN. *(overlap)* IAN.

IAN. No I mean it! Is she kidding? Are you kidding me? Because I'm just appalled, really, that you give yourself permission to say things like that, and I'm not talking about being called self-centered, nasty, none of it. That's not what really appalls me, in your, it's not even an argument, it's just blather, "More than half the world believes in god?" Not very long ago everybody believed that the earth was the center of the universe and the sun rode in Apollo's golden chariot through the morning sky. Half the world believes in god, big deal, half the world are fecking eejits –

PETER. Seriously –

MAUREEN. He's drunk –

IAN. I'm not so drunk I can't be appalled by rampant stupidity.

(a beat)

MAUREEN. You never got curtains for this room did you? Did you look at blinds? There are these new blinds I saw, somewhere, they are so easy to use you just touch them and they go up, it's a miracle!

PETER. Really?

MAUREEN. I remember where I saw them, in Ariel's apartment, do you remember, Ian? She has them in the back bedroom, they're kind of a putty color, or clay, you know one of those sort of grays that has a lot of brown and green in it. Taupe. I would call it taupe. Very very neutral, you don't even notice them. You get both light and privacy, I was thinking about getting some for our kitchen, in something that has a little more yellow in it. Nothing too bright, you always want to stay neutral with blinds. Butter. Anyway Ariel just loves them. Ian you liked them, remember?

IAN. I don't actually.

MAUREEN. You do too you loved them! At least you said you did. We both did. We really both just thought they were terrific.

PETER. Great we'll look into that then.

MAUREEN. You should. You really should.

PETER. Have you thought where you'd like to sleep? We're in the back bedroom upstairs so you can take the front. Or the one off the den. Although Ella doesn't like the bed in that room.

MAUREEN. Really why not?

PETER. She finds the bedding a bit heavy I think isn't that what you said, El?

MAUREEN. I love that bedspread. It's so pretty, the lavender and periwinkle, I don't think it's heavy at all.

PETER. Not the colors, the bedding. She gets hot. Her feet get hot.

MAUREEN. But you don't sleep in there.

PETER. Not often. Now and then. It's all yours if you like.

MAUREEN. I love that room. This whole place. This would be a terrific house for kids, why didn't you ever have kids, Peter? You would be such a good father.

PETER. Great. I'm gonna go up, you coming, Ella?

ELLA. No.

MAUREEN. Well I'm going to bed. Come on, Ian.

IAN. I'm not really very tired.

MAUREEN. It's after midnight! Really, it's gotten so that I just can't drink anymore. Three glasses of wine and I'm done for.

IAN. So the six you had tonight have most certainly taken their toll.

> *(beat)*

Are you staying or going?

MAUREEN. I'm going. Good night, Peter.

> *(She goes. A beat.)*

PETER. I'm going up too. Are you coming?

ELLA. No.

> *(She drinks.)*

PETER. Well. Don't drink too much.

ELLA. Don't tell me what to do, please.

PETER. I just meant, it makes it so hard for you to sleep.

> *(After a beat, he goes. **ELLA** takes off her earrings and rubs her earlobes. **IAN** reaches for the bottle of wine.)*

IAN. Yes?

ELLA. By dismissing all notions of right and wrong as beneath discussion, you leave the field open to the people you claim to despise the most.

IAN. They are welcome to it.

ELLA. Consequently you dismiss as well, the most startling and significant events of human history. If Irish poetry isn't good; if Yosemite Valley is not beautiful –

IAN. Yosemite Valley… Let me tell you a thing or two about your Yosemite Valley. All the way back, whenever that was no one knew it was there. Except for the Indians. You weren't allow to talk about it, 'specially not to the white man. Off limits. It's a secret. Until one night, finally, there's a fight, isn't there, people going at each other in a general store, over dry goods or some such. Madness. A couple local Indians do something stupid, they murder and scalp the poor man owns the store, his wife and child, the same carnage. Listen to me, this is a true story I'm telling now. Blood on their hands, these red indians. They flee into the High Sierra where they think, we're safe here from the soldiers sent after them because no one knew it was there, this holy valley. But the soldiers found them, didn't they, they came over the mountains, found the valley, and then they slaughtered every man woman and child who lived there and most of these brilliant military men didn't even look at it. They were too busy killing redskins to see it, all but one. One benighted officer who in the middle of the bloodshed did look around and think Jaysus, this feckin place, and that spawned a train of tourists which today crowds the roads and poisons the air of that apocalyptic fantasyland, so no. I do not think the word "beautiful" covers, rightly, what Yosemite Valley is.

ELLA. Thank you for the history lesson.

IAN. You're welcome.

ELLA. And thank you also for pointing out the subtle misuse of the word "beautiful" by those of us who are tossing it about so recklessly these days.

IAN. Anybody wants to talk to me about god, I'd be happy to set you all straight on that as well.

ELLA. Then you clarify something for me. Since when is morality the same thing as semiotics?

IAN. I'm sorry did you just say 'semiotics?'

ELLA. Yes I used a big word, it is possible once in a while. Answer the question.

IAN. What was the question? I'm still reeling from the big word.

ELLA. Since when are semiotics and morality the same thing?

IAN. Oh my god, you're still mad at me for making fun of Mr. Smith.

ELLA. No. No. Maybe.

    (embarrassed)

Why does arguing for simple human decency make people sound stupid?

IAN. It doesn't.

ELLA. Shut up.

IAN. I don't even know what we're on about anymore.

ELLA. This is what it was.

IAN. Stop. Your argument is simply muddled beyond redemption – oh and now we have "redemption" something else you're probably going to want to plug in somewhere in this endlessly incoherent point you're trying to make.

ELLA. You're the one who said redemption, not me!

IAN. So what, you started this.

ELLA. And you don't even remember how, do you?

IAN. Of course I do.

ELLA. What was it then?

IAN. You know, oh god, it was just so pedestrian –

ELLA. You don't remember.

IAN. Yes I do.

ELLA. No, you were too busy tearing it down to even consider it. You didn't even hear it.

IAN. I heard it; I'm just too drunk to remember it.

ELLA. You don't remember it because you dismissed it out of hand. You presuppose there is no elegant argument for goodness. You presuppose that a corrupted and hypocritical and even hysterical distortion of morality is the real thing, which is shoddy logic at best.

IAN. *(caught by the truth of this)* Oh.

ELLA. Dismissing the perversion is not in fact the same thing as dismissing the actual thing.

IAN. Yes, I see.

ELLA. It's like dismissing the possibility of compassion in the universe because institutional religion doesn't understand it and never did.

IAN. Well –

ELLA. It's just nonsense. We don't live in a hideous and broken world, we live in a beautiful world. Not perfect but beautiful. Yosemite Valley IS beautiful. Irish poetry is beautiful. People are beautiful.

> *(He looks at her.)*

ELLA. They are!

IAN. My father always said that. Truth be told, that's why I know such an annoying amount of useless facts about Yosemite. He had so many books about it. It was his dream to go there.

ELLA. I always liked your dad. How he spawned you I will never know.

IAN. He liked you too.

ELLA. How's he doing?

> *(She goes to the sink, taking the last wine glasses.)*

IAN. Oh. You know – sorry. Sorry, I should have told you. He, ah, he died.

ELLA. What?

IAN. He died. About a month ago, actually. Six weeks?

ELLA. Your father died?

IAN. Yes.

ELLA. Ian.

IAN. It's a good thing. He was filled with the cancer. It was everywhere. His brain –

ELLA. Oh.

IAN. He was in a lot of pain. Or so I'm told. I didn't – ah. I didn't actually make it over to see him.

ELLA. You didn't see him?

(She doesn't know what to say. He is clearly in pain.)

IAN. He still lives, lived in Donegal, out in that village halfway to nowhere. It takes a day and a half to get there. Maureen felt she couldn't spare me. No one thought he'd go that fast. I thought I had time, to talk her into it. I should have just gone. To hell with it, why didn't I just go? And then I didn't go to the funeral either! I didn't want to see them bury him, I – and Maureen – fuck it, no, I didn't want to see them bury him, anyway, it was too late by then. I should have gone. He was out there, in that shitty hospital. Alone.

(then)

What I really should have done was take him to Yosemite Valley. That's what I should have done.

(There is a terrible pause. He gasps for air, at the admission. She goes to him, puts her arms around him, and holds him. He shakes for a moment, holding his sobs. He finally stops. She pulls away, looks at him. They are still holding each other. He smiles at her, touches her hair. It is truly too intimate. Behind him, MAUREEN appears on the stair.)

MAUREEN. I'm sorry. I didn't mean to interrupt.

ELLA. Oh, Maureen.

IAN. Not interrupting. Not at all. Good night.

ELLA. Good night.

> *(He leaves, quick, passing* MAUREEN *on the stair. She shoots* ELLA *a look — what was that? — and then follows.* ELLA *sighs, goes to the counter. Lights shift and she goes to bed.)*

> *(Lights shift again.* IAN *comes downstairs. It is early. He looks around the empty kitchen, sees* ELLA*'s earrings on the table. He sits, picks them up and looks at them.)*

> *(*MAUREEN *enters, in a beautiful robe over pajamas. She stares at him.)*

MAUREEN. You're up early.

> *(*IAN *closes his hands over the earrings, sudden, casually pockets them.)*

IAN. What time is it?

MAUREEN. Seven. You tossed all night.

IAN. Are you making coffee, I'd love some.

MAUREEN. Something bothering you?

IAN. Well, I drank four bottles of wine last night, which wasn't bothering me then but seems to be now. I have a whanging hangover. There are muffins somewhere.

MAUREEN. Are there?

IAN. You know there are. We stopped and bought them at that atrocious store, where everything is so original.

> *(He starts to look around.)*

MAUREEN. If you didn't want to buy the muffins I don't know why we stopped –

IAN. Well I didn't actually want to buy the muffins, I thought the muffins were ridiculously indulgent in their definition, "ginger blueberry tomato confit", "peach mango peppercorn," Christ it makes your head split –

MAUREEN. No one was begging you –

IAN. In fact you were begging me to buy the muffins, and I did so gladly; that does not excuse the horrendous excess of their composition.

MAUREEN. I never know what you're talking about half the time.

IAN. I'm talking about the fact that I could really use a muffin. I got completely smashed last night and if I don't get something in my stomach I'm going to puke my feckin brains out all over the floor of our dear friends's kitchen.

MAUREEN. The muffins are still in the car.

IAN. Ah.

(He goes to the door.)

MAUREEN. Are you just going to walk out?

IAN. What?

MAUREEN. You are, you're just going to walk away from me.

IAN. You said they were in the car.

MAUREEN. You're ridiculous.

IAN. That I know.

MAUREEN. Just say it!

(pause)

SAY IT.

IAN. You know honestly people are not usually begging me to speak in my experience usually people tend to beg me to shut up so why don't you –

MAUREEN. You think I don't KNOW? EVERYBODY knows. You aren't exactly the world's most subtle person.

IAN. I never claimed to be the world's most subtle person. It's not actually one of my life's goals.

MAUREEN. I would like to KILL you.

(the briefest of silences)

IAN. That would of course solve a few things while in addition providing a certain amount of personal satisfaction. However, unless you do in fact intend to proceed down some vaguely premeditated path, I do want to reiterate that I'm tired and I am not now nor have I ever been particularly interested in hysterics and in addition I got really drunk last night and now find that I want a FECKING MUFFIN. So I'm going out to the car, now, and I'm going to get a fecking muffin. Is that all right with you? Is it?

MAUREEN. As if you care what's "all right" with me.

IAN. I'll bring the whole bag, shall I? Terrific.

> *(He goes. She stands, immobile for a moment, then starts to cry. She leans over, sobbing, then stands up, again furious, overwhelmed with emotion. IAN returns.)*

They're not in the car, we must have brought them in. Oh god.

> *(He sees her sobbing.)*

Stop it. Now stop it. Maureen, I'm serious. You've got to stop.

> *(He goes to her, tries to help her calm down. She shoves him away.)*

MAUREEN. Leave me alone.

IAN. Do you want a muffin? They've got to be here somewhere.

MAUREEN. My mother said this would happen.

IAN. Okay.

MAUREEN. She said – she said –

IAN. Before we get into this might I remind you that she has been dead for eight years?

MAUREEN. She said you would turn out to be a liar and a cheater, she told me before we were even married.

IAN. Yes I miss her too.

MAUREEN. It was all about the green card. She said that! It was really what you wanted –

IAN. Jesus Christ do you even hear yourself?

MAUREEN. I could have had anybody! I had three marriage proposals before I was out of college, I was pursued – YOU pursued me, and I believed you, even though even though –

IAN. I am not doing this, Maureen.

MAUREEN. I'm not doing it either!

IAN. Good. Because it's highly unpleasant.

MAUREEN. *(raising her voice)* I want a divorce. I want out of this. I want it to be over.

IAN. Where are those muffins?

MAUREEN. That's all you have to say?

IAN. What is it you want me to say? Why don't you say whatever it is that you want to say? What is it you want to know?

MAUREEN. Are you sleeping with her?

> *(a pause)*

Just say it. You're sleeping with her. I know anyway.

IAN. If you know it anyway, why do you need me to say it.

MAUREEN. I want you to say it!

IAN. You want me to say it.

MAUREEN. Yes.

IAN. I don't believe that to be true.

MAUREEN. We're in their house! You brought me to their house – And you flaunt it in front of both of us –

IAN. I'm not flaunting anything.

MAUREEN. All night –

> *(The argument explodes; they speak on top of each other.)*

IAN. So what is, what is it that you presume I'm doing –

MAUREEN. *(overlapping)* You presume you do presume –

IAN. *(overlapping)* When and what, aside from screaming at each other –

MAUREEN. *(overlapping)* You presume that I am going to put up with this shit indefinitely but I'm NOT you asshole –

IAN. *(overlapping)* Because honestly that is all that happened –

MAUREEN. *(overlapping)* There isn't even a shred of, you're deliberately humiliating me now and it's not it's not –

IAN. *(overlapping)* And in fact, I ask you to do me the favor, please have the dignity to admit –

MAUREEN. *(overlapping)* Anything I can't I cannot live with this anymore

IAN. *(overlapping)* That it was your idea to even come. As you well know. I didn't want to come, I find these weekend outings insufferable –

MAUREEN. *(overlapping)* The contempt the indifference the CONTEMPT –

IAN. And I am not in the best of shape right now AS YOU WELL KNOW. As you well know I said very clearly I don't want to see them, I'm tired and sad as my father just recently –

MAUREEN. Don't throw that at me, that's cheap –

IAN. Cheap. Good god above. It's cheap to mention –

MAUREEN. How was I supposed to know he was going to die? And you know what, I don't fully believe he IS dead. There wasn't a funeral, you didn't go to a funeral, and it's not out of the question that you would just would just –

IAN. Christ above, I need a break and I don't want to be here. I didn't want to be here and I do not want to be here now.

MAUREEN. And now we know why. I know why. I saw it last night. I saw you – in her arms –

IAN. Christ.

MAUREEN. *(beat)* Say it.

> *(He looks at her, shrugs.)*

IAN. I don't deny it.

MAUREEN. You fucking asshole.

IAN. Well –

*(She throws an empty bottle of wine at him. He ducks. It hits the wall, then falls. He looks at her. After a moment, **PETER** enters, worried.)*

PETER. Everything okay?

IAN. We brought some muffins, I couldn't find them.

PETER. Oh.

IAN. They're probably still in the car. I mean, I looked, I did look. Guess I'll look again.

*(He goes. Silence. **PETER** looks at **MAUREEN**, who does not look at him.)*

PETER. Is there coffee?

*(She goes, into the house. He thinks about this, starts to make coffee. After a moment, **ELLA** pokes her head in.)*

ELLA. How is it?

PETER. All clear.

ELLA. Thank god. Holy shit, did she throw something at him?

PETER. She threw a wine bottle at him.

ELLA. Shit.

(She enters, cautious, looks around, then goes to the refrigerator and takes out a bottle of seltzer while he makes coffee.)

Did you hear what they were arguing about?

PETER. I was doing my best not to.

ELLA. *(whispering)* His father died.

PETER. What?

ELLA. His father died a couple months ago and she wouldn't let him go.

PETER. She wouldn't let him.

ELLA. She's crazy. Crazy.

PETER. *(laughing)* Shhhh.

ELLA. Seriously that's what he told me! god. I have such a hangover. My head is about to explode.

PETER. I told you.

ELLA. I know you told me; I know. And you know, I knew she was crazy, but not letting him go say goodbye to his dying father? That's beyond, that's just –

PETER. Why didn't he go anyway?

ELLA. I don't know Peter but seriously he's a wreck about it.

PETER. He didn't sound like a wreck. Oh. Here's the muffins.

(He finds them; opens the bag, starts to take them out, while **ELLA** *takes some aspirin.)*

ELLA. What's the hangover thing you're supposed to do? A raw egg with beer or something?

PETER. I don't think so.

ELLA. An egg and something. Ginger ale?

PETER. That's disgusting.

ELLA. Well it's supposed to be. Beer with an egg in it. I saw it in a movie.

PETER. Oh if you saw it in a movie by all means. What is this, tomatoes?

ELLA. Tomato juice? You think it's tomato juice and a raw egg? Who could get that down?

PETER. No, tomatoes in the muffins.

(He eats.)

ELLA. No that can't be.

(She looks at the muffin. He doesn't like it, gives it to her while he tries another.)

PETER. It is, there's tomatoes in the muffins. Wait not in all of them.

ELLA. Tomato muffins. People have too much time on their hands.

PETER. *(looking toward the door)* Do you think we should do anything?

ELLA. Like what?

PETER. I don't know.

ELLA. I can't believe they even came. This whole thing with Ian's father is sad and awful, really, they belong in a therapist's office, not flitting around the countryside. I told you not to invite them.

PETER. His father dying is hardly my fault.

ELLA. Of course it wasn't, oh for heaven's sake. But you know, they're never fun.

(She tries another muffin.)

PETER. You were having fun last night.

ELLA. I was drunk. I'm still drunk. These muffins are disgusting. What is in this?

(She takes some out of her mouth and puts it back on the table.)

PETER. For god's sake you can't just – what are you, a child?

(He goes, gets a napkin and cleans up the muffin.)

ELLA. Well it's horrible.

(She starts to open another muffin.)

PETER. Would you stop it? You're going to ruin all the muffins.

ELLA. I just want to find one that's edible. god there's pepper in this one. Why can't people make decent muffins anymore. Not like boring muffins, bran muffins, that wasn't a good idea, even with the raisins there was nothing really appealing about a bran muffin, or a CORN muffin, but remember when they were like just, you know, pumpkin. Or those green muffins, pistachio, those were delicious. Chocolate. There was a minute there when people were making chocolate muffins now that was a good idea. Ow my head hurts. I could use a chocolate muffin.

PETER. I could run into town and get some.

ELLA. No. You are not leaving me here, alone with them. Why did you invite them? They always do this. She loses her marbles over nothing and everything gets all tense and unpleasant. And you know the story, that she tried to…

(She mimes downing a bottle of pills, starts to look for her earrings.)

PETER. Tried to what?

ELLA. You know.

PETER. She's always been high strung.

ELLA. She took a bunch of pills!

PETER. You don't know that for a fact.

ELLA. You visited her in the hospital and you told me, Peter.

PETER. That was food poisoning.

ELLA. Food poisoning. Please. Everybody says I've got food poisoning when it just means you have a hangover. Or, you tried to kill yourself. You know what?
That's probably why he didn't go to see his father on his deathbed, because she threatened to give it another go. I wouldn't put it past her.

PETER. She's not that bad.

ELLA. Oh. Really?

PETER. All I'm saying is, they're here, so…

ELLA. I know they're here, they're in our house! Why did we invite them? Why did we decide not to have kids?

PETER. What?

ELLA. That's the problem with not having kids. You have to hang out with other couples with no kids. That's why they're here. That's why we're stuck with them. They just they show up and everything, just everything is suddenly in question.

PETER. What do you mean in question?

ELLA. Nothing. I'm sorry. Look. They're your friends.

PETER. They're OUR friends.

ELLA. You knew them first.

PETER. You got me. I knew them first.

ELLA. Well, I think we should just tell them to go.

PETER. Ella. The man's father died. And she's almost family.

ELLA. She's not! I know your brother wanted to marry her, but he didn't, thank god and that was ages ago and they should, this isn't a good weekend.

PETER. This isn't entirely their fault.

ELLA. Oh for crying out loud. Meaning what, what's your point? You want me to apologize? I was really nice to him last night when he told me about his dad. He's not mad at me, I know he's not.

PETER. Not him.

ELLA. Oh. Really?

PETER. Is there a problem?

ELLA. What is this, kindergarten?

PETER. Forget it.

ELLA. I'm sorry. You told me to stop drinking and I didn't and now I'm just behaving like a jerk. I'm sorry.

PETER. You're not behaving like a jerk.

ELLA. Yes I am and I actually was kind of horrible to you last night too. I'm sorry.

PETER. It's okay.

ELLA. Don't be so nice about it Peter, honestly –

PETER. Are you going to pick a fight with me now because I'm being too nice to you?

> *(She hugs him again. He holds her for a moment, then she moves away from him, restless.)*

ELLA. Sorry. Sorry. And now I'm being all clingy.

PETER. Are you all right?

ELLA. I'm just hungover. So now what is this plan, you think I should apologize, to Maureen?

PETER. I don't think it would hurt.

ELLA. It might. She doesn't exactly excel at accepting apologies.

PETER. Is that why you give them? To give the other person a chance to excel?

ELLA. Oh god please –

PETER. Forget it then.

(MAUREEN *re-enters.*)

There you are!

ELLA. *(covering instantly)* Maureen! How are you? I have a whanging hangover.

MAUREEN. I'm not surprised.

ELLA. Me neither. Wow. I am so sorry I drank so much last night. And I'm – you know I'm really sorry, I have to apologize about last night I don't know what came over me.

MAUREEN. You and Ian apparently had things you needed to get off your chest...

ELLA. Well. No. I just... I. You know. Anyway. I'm sorry, I really am.

MAUREEN. What for?

ELLA. Well I was just – drunk!

MAUREEN. That's what you're sorry for?

ELLA. Yes. And for fighting. That was really, oh boy. I am so sorry. And I was really sorry to hear about Ian's father.

MAUREEN. *(very cold)* Oh, he told you about that, did he?

(She looks at PETER, *helpless in the face of this.)*

ELLA. He did, and we were both... Sorry to hear about it.

MAUREEN. I'm sure.

PETER. You want some coffee, Maureen? We found the muffins you guys brought, they were somehow inexplicably stuck in a drawer. Ella unfortunately stuck her fingers in well all of them, but if we excavate around those sections I think some of them are salvageable.

(He starts to take a knife to the muffins.)

ELLA. *(laughing)* I couldn't find one that I liked.

MAUREEN. So you destroyed them all.

ELLA. I didn't mean to.

MAUREEN. I'm sure.

PETER. There's eggs. Why don't I make some eggs?

ELLA. None for me. I'm going to take a shower.

(She goes. **PETER**, *at the sink, starts to cook.)*

PETER. Maureen? You want some scrambled eggs?

*(***MAUREEN** *sits, starts to cry.)*

Oh. Oh, Maureen, I'm sorry, are are you all right?

MAUREEN. No. I... I'm so sorry. This is, really, it's...

PETER. Let me get you some coffee. We didn't do that yet, did we?

MAUREEN. Ian...

PETER. It's all right. You're all right.

MAUREEN. He told me that he he he –

PETER. He's probably really sad right now.

MAUREEN. You know what he told me.

PETER. Just upset.

MAUREEN. He and Ella. He told me.

(a beat)

PETER. Seriously, Maureen, I'm sure he'll be fine. It just takes a little while, to get over a loss like that.

MAUREEN. I'm not talking about that!

PETER. Well.

MAUREEN. You know what I'm talking about.

PETER. No, I don't.

MAUREEN. It never occurred to you.

PETER. Here, these muffins are good.

MAUREEN. Are you going to make me say it?

PETER. I'm not going to make you say anything.

MAUREEN. But you know. I can see it in your face, you know. You've known for a long time. I've known for a long time, how could I not? And then last night, the way they went at each other. In front of us. In front of us both!

PETER. You know, Maureen. Obviously you and Ian are having a little bit of a hard time right now, and maybe this wasn't the right time for a visit.

MAUREEN. He told me that he and Ella are having an affair. Is that what you mean by a hard time?

PETER. *(beat)* I guess that would fall under that category.

MAUREEN. You don't care?

PETER. Well, I don't – actually – believe it, Maureen.

MAUREEN. So last night struck you as "normal."

PETER. Last night struck me as "drunk," is what last night struck me as. And you know Ella apologized because she feels bad, she really –

MAUREEN. Oh I know how bad she feels.

PETER. Well she does, she told me –

MAUREEN. Did she tell you that I walked in on them?

PETER. You walked in on them?

MAUREEN. In each other's arms. Last night. After you and I went to bed, they were –

PETER. Hang on.

MAUREEN. They were in each other's arms!

PETER. Were their clothes on?

MAUREEN. They were – it was – and then I confronted them, this morning, and he told me. He told me they were sleeping together.

PETER. Currently? Like, right now?

MAUREEN. We didn't get into specifics! He said they were sleeping together, that's as specific as we got!

PETER. And he told you this –

MAUREEN. This morning! He stood right here, in this kitchen and told me, he he he told me – I asked him and he said yes. He said they were –

PETER. I heard you the first time.

MAUREEN. That's all you have to say?

PETER. Well I don't believe it Maureen!

MAUREEN. Don't you?

PETER. No, I don't. I don't.

MAUREEN. I do.

PETER. Well, that's your prerogative.

MAUREEN. Ask her.

PETER. No, thank you, I am not going to ask my wife is she having an affair with your husband.

MAUREEN. Are you afraid of the answer?

PETER. Afraid? No, actually, I'm – annoyed now, I think we could say that I am in fact annoyed. But I'm not afraid of the answer to a question I am not going to ask.

MAUREEN. Then I'll ask her.

PETER. I don't think that's a good idea.

MAUREEN. Of course you don't.

PETER. Listen, we invited you up for the weekend as friends, you know we're friends!

MAUREEN. Who do you think it happens to, strangers?

PETER. I don't think – it happens – to me. Honestly. I don't know what happens beyond that but it is not happening here; it is not happening to either one of us. Come on.

MAUREEN. If you're so sure then asking her shouldn't be a problem.

PETER. That is precisely why it is a problem.

MAUREEN. You make no sense. None of this, it doesn't make any –

PETER. Look. Ella actually, had already suggested that maybe you should –

MAUREEN. If you don't mind I don't particularly want to hear what Ella has to say about this! Is that all right with you?

PETER. What I meant to say was, I'm sorry you're having such a hard time. And Ian's father, dying –

MAUREEN. Don't bring that in. It's a complete lie.

PETER. His father didn't die?

MAUREEN. He's such a liar. He lies about everything. You can't tell what the truth is. You can't even tell.

(She starts to cry again.)

PETER. Maybe you should talk to Ian.

MAUREEN. That's what I'm saying, you can't talk to him!

PETER. Okay, but you know, we can't be involved in this.

MAUREEN. You are involved! At least Ella is!

PETER. Maureen, come on...

MAUREEN. If you want to ignore what is going on right under your own nose that would be your choice, but don't tell me you're not involved!

(She is crying now, sobbing.)

PETER. Oh boy. Maybe you should lie down.

MAUREEN. It won't help.

PETER. It will. I promise.

MAUREEN. We should have had kids.

PETER. Come on. Let's go lie down. You'll feel better in a little while.

> *(He takes the sobbing woman off. After a moment, IAN enters the empty kitchen, looks around. He sees the muffins; eats one. Dislikes it. Spits it out and takes another which is also terrible. As he's spitting out the second one, PETER reenters.)*

IAN. These muffins are disgusting.

PETER. Well, you don't just spit them out! You and Ella, you both...

> *(He stops himself, then goes to pick up the plate of muffins, which he takes to the sink.)*

IAN. Ella and I both what?

PETER. Nothing. I just don't know why you'd bring muffins that nobody can eat.

IAN. Are you angry?

PETER. Am I, Jesus. Are you kidding?

IAN. Look, I'm sorry about Maureen. You know how she gets.

PETER. Yes she seems very upset.

IAN. That's polite.

PETER. She's lying down.

IAN. Good.

PETER. You don't want to go talk to her?

IAN. What do you think?

PETER. I think it might help.

IAN. Well then you talk to her.

PETER. I did.

IAN. Did it help?

PETER. No actually it –

IAN. Which would be my point. Talking her down does no good at all; she gets herself right back up there at the drop of a hat.

PETER. This is different.

IAN. Different than what?

PETER. I think maybe you should take her home.

(There is an uncomfortable pause at this.)

IAN. Could I have some coffee? Is there nothing to eat, really, other than these abysmal muffins? Is there any tea?

*(**PETER** sighs, turns to the cabinet, opens it and brings out a package of Lipton tea. He hands it to **IAN**, then goes back to the counter. **IAN** looks at it, sets it down.)*

PETER. If you like I could scramble you up some eggs.

IAN. Not if it's any trouble.

PETER. Look, I'm not, could you please not – just ignore what I'm saying here? This is, this situation is difficult, Ian, it's really really difficult and I'm not kidding, I think, I did say, to Maureen, as well, I think that this is, well, I don't know what you're going through, you two, but this is clearly not the right time. Last night I don't know what was going on, with you and Ella –

IAN. We were drunk and we were having an argument.

PETER. Well you know Maureen is real upset now –

IAN. She's always upset; you know this, and you invited her anyway, so –

PETER. You know what she said. Do you know what she said to me?

IAN. She doesn't believe my father died.

PETER. That's part of it.

IAN. He did though. Just for the record.

PETER. Okay. As I said, I'm really sorry to hear about that and that's part of my point, Ian. That's not the only unusual thing that Maureen said. She said some other things too.

IAN. What other things?

PETER. Well. Well. She said that she thinks you and Ella are – somehow – involved with each other in an inappropriate way –

IAN. Maureen said that Ella and I were inappropriate? That's a laugh. She's the most consistently inappropriate person I've ever met, you should hear the things she accuses me of, on a daily basis.

PETER. I have heard what she accuses you of. I have heard one specific thing that she's accused you of, and I also have heard that you didn't deny it.

(a beat)

IAN. Are you asking me a question?

PETER. How about if I just ask you to leave. I'm not getting involved in this.

IAN. You're asking me to leave.

PETER. Yes.

IAN. Why? Because my wife told you something? My wife who everyone knows is completely raving bonkers, the women is an emotional lunatic from start to finish, you told me yourself, at our engagement party, the night we were celebrating our engagement you were drunk and you said to me, that you've known her your entire life and you think she's crackers.

PETER. I don't recall that but –

IAN. Yes yes yes, I'm told we've GOT to invite you because of your poor sad lovesick brother, I don't know you and I could give a shit about your brother, frankly, I've just got engaged to a woman who at the time I found honestly delightful, I did, I was in love with her and America too truth be told, why not, America looks great when you're young and sick of Europe. So cheers, I'm going to marry a terrific American girl, we're toasting to my upcoming nuptials in some total stranger's kitchen and you just blurt it, you come out and tell me in no uncertain terms that I will regret marrying her because she's a lunatic.

PETER. I don't remember this conversation.

IAN. And I married her anyway and you're right, she's insane, and we've talked about it many times since, you and I, over drinks, at dinners and cocktail parties, never so explicitly, "how is it being married to that completely insane woman, you know I warned you!" More subtle than that but not much, you've always been really rather smug about it truth be told. No you have! Because you have Ella. And I have Maureen. Which always made me wonder. When she'd come home and say, oh guess what good news Peter and Ella have asked us up to their house for the weekend, won't that be grand. The question really is grand for whom?

PETER. I'm not all that sure what your point is, Ian.

IAN. Really? I think I'm being awfully clear. Almost offensively so.

PETER. Well, I think I'm being pretty clear, too. I think this is not a good time for any of us, and it would be better for everyone if you and Maureen just went back to the city.

IAN. Why do you want us to leave?

PETER. Come on, Ian –

IAN. No, seriously, I ask because honestly Peter I don't think it's a good idea, I sincerely don't. You want us to

leave because Ella and I had a silly, drunken argument
last night?

PETER. I want you to leave because Maureen has made this
reckless accusation and now she's in there losing it –

IAN. And if I go in there and tell Maureen "we're leaving"
she will immediately take that as affirmation, that she
is right, that her insane accusations about me and Ella
have more than a shred of truth and she's landed spot
on it –

PETER. Didn't you already tell her that?

IAN. That's the second time you've asked me that – it's
really bothering you, isn't it?

> (**PETER** *looks at him. There is a rather dreadful
> silence while both men consider what* **PETER** *might
> do next.* **ELLA** *enters, from the stair. Her hair is
> wet. She wears a small t shirt and sweatpants and
> she is very moist overall.*)

ELLA. Well, I feel much better. god the showers are good
in this house. I can't stand our shower in the city, the
water is never hot enough and there's no water pressure
at all; it is truly just a thoroughly useless shower and
then you just get used to it and then you come up here
and go my god why have I been putting up with that
lousy shower? We have to talk to the super again, or
even bring it up with the co-op board.

PETER. *(a slight pause)* They're not going to completely
redo the plumbing in the building because you want
more water pressure, Ella.

ELLA. It's not just the water pressure, it's the temperature
too, and the fact is we pay maintenance fees like
everybody else. Exactly the same fee and you know
those people on the first and second floor have terrific
showers. I don't think it's fair. We should leave that
building. I know you love it there, but we've been
married for how long, and I've always hated the
doorman, and it still feels like your apartment, and
I'm just going to say it – the people on our floor suck.

Seriously, they are all so mean in the elevators. Good god, Ian, what are you doing with that? Peter, you didn't give him this, tell me you didn't.

> *(She takes the box of tea from* **IAN**, *who pulls it back for a moment, teasing her, before he lets her take it.)*

PETER. He asked for tea.

IAN. I did I asked Peter for a cup of tea, he gave me the box.

ELLA. You gave him this? Why do we even have this, it's completely undrinkable.

PETER. It's all we have.

ELLA. No, I stopped at the tea and coffee place up on 83rd, and got some of the real stuff, – here it is –

> *(She reaches into a cupboard and gets out a box of proper tea.)*

IAN. You bought tea for me? That was lovely of you.

ELLA. Well god you can't drink that other stuff, I can't believe we even have that. Peter, did you put water on?

PETER. No.

ELLA. Well how is that supposed to work. He asks for tea, so you hand him a box of this pretend tea, and then no one puts water on? This whole weekend is a disaster.

PETER. I was just saying the same thing.

> *(She goes to the sink and pours water in a kettle, puts it on the stove and starts to make tea as they talk.)*

IAN. I don't think it's a disaster, I think it's kind of interesting.

ELLA. You would. And there's still nothing to eat I'm guessing, those muffins have finally disappeared thank goodness.

IAN. Yes I did them in I'm afraid.

ELLA. You ate them?

IAN. No, I just more or less destroyed them.

ELLA. Good they were horrible. Maybe I'll run into town and go to that little bakery, get some sort of croissant things, with almond paste or cheese or something.

IAN. Chocolate.

ELLA. Well a chocolate muffin would be ideal but I doubt that they have them. They're too bourgeois I think for this place.

IAN. More bourgeois than croissant?

ELLA. You know, whatever the word is for not cool enough.

IAN. I'll come with you, shall I?

PETER. I thought you were leaving.

(a beat)

ELLA. Are you? Leaving?

IAN. There's been some talk of it.

ELLA. Oh.

PETER. Maureen's not feeling well.

ELLA. Well, no I know that.

IAN. Peter thought it best that we take off.

ELLA. He did.

IAN. Yes.

ELLA. Why?

PETER. Well, because we're all upset. Just everything, nothing actually seems, we're upset so...

ELLA. Yeah but aren't we like mostly upset because there's nothing for breakfast?

PETER. Actually El I think people are a little more upset than that. Certainly Maureen is.

ELLA. And she wants to go home? Did she say that?

IAN. She did not actually say that.

PETER. However, she is spectacularly upset –

ELLA. Because of the fight we had? She wasn't even in the fight. I mean, I was barely in the fight, I was so drunk.

IAN. This is my position. I absolutely apologize for the amount of alcohol I consumed last night. My entire being apologizes. My entire being also does not particularly feel like getting into a car for two and a half hours. All things being equal.

ELLA. Did you get any aspirin, or has anyone offered you beer with an egg in it?

IAN. Not precisely.

PETER. We don't have any beer.

ELLA. I can get some, when I go for pastries. I'm going to have to make a list. Maybe you should take a shower at least, Ian, the water is really hot here and I don't know I think it may have steamed the hangover right out of me.

IAN. Maybe I'll try that.

ELLA. Do you need towels?

IAN. I'll let you know.

> *(He smiles, stands and goes.* **PETER** *looks at* **ELLA** *like she's an idiot.)*

ELLA. What?

PETER. I thought you wanted them to leave! I just spent the last twenty minutes trying to convince them to leave, and now you're begging them to stay?

ELLA. I was hardly "begging."

PETER. You were saying "please stay." I was saying because you told me and now you're all let's have muffins and eggs!

ELLA. Well I feel bad.

PETER. You feel bad?

ELLA. You were the one who said I was acting bad!

PETER. Okay okay –

ELLA. So I took a shower and sobered up and I thought about what you said and I do, I feel bad, I think I behaved really poorly last night and you're right, we invited them up for the weekend and they're having a hard time, and now what, we're going to send them home because Ian and I got into a stupid fight?

PETER. This is alarmingly inconsistent.

ELLA. Oh well then. Let's burn me at the stake.

PETER. Okay look. You were right. This is, they should go home.

ELLA. Do you really want to send them careening down the Taconic after the night we had last night? You were right, it was as much my fault as anything, what happened, more even, I know I sat here and whined about how horrible Ian is but I was the one who was just out of control. I just was on some kind of rampage, that's hardly their fault and if now we're like oh you have to leave now, I would have to say that we are the ones who behaved poorly. Not them.

PETER. I actually cannot follow this.

ELLA. I'm saying you were right. Come on, you love that, when I say that.

PETER. Do you know what she said? Maureen?

ELLA. Something psychotic I'm sure, she's always saying something horrible about someone. I know you like her but you ask me, she's a lot of work. What did she say?

(a pause)

PETER. Forget it.

ELLA. Well, now I don't know what to think. I mean – I don't know why you're so loyal to her, if it upsets you this much to see her.

PETER. You were the one who said. Have them up. You know, you were the one who actually said we should have them up. It was your idea Ella.

ELLA. No it wasn't.

PETER. We saw them at that auction thing and you said why don't you come up, you haven't been up for so long. To Ian. You said it to Ian.

ELLA. Well I don't remember.

PETER. You said it.

ELLA. I don't remember, besides it doesn't –

PETER. You said it and then Maureen called me, at work, and said we should look at our calendars and figure out a weekend. She said Ian said his schedule was going to get tight and we should figure it out sooner rather than later or it wouldn't happen. That is why they are here.

ELLA. What are you so bent out of shape about?

PETER. I am bent out of shape because you and Ian you – both –

> *(IAN sticks his head through the door. PETER stops.)*

IAN. Oh sorry. Everything all right?

PETER. Yes. Just this is all a little. Sorry.

IAN. I just wanted to let you know that I did speak with Maureen and she's feeling a lot better. A little embarrassed, actually. About something she said.

PETER. Well, that's fine, but –

IAN. She'd like to apologize.

PETER. That's not necessary.

IAN. She's rather anxious actually.

> *(a beat)*

PETER. I thought you said she was feeling better.

IAN. She feels better but she also feels anxious and she'd like to apologize.

PETER. Meaning what?

IAN. I don't know Peter; why is this so difficult? Meaning, can you go in there so she can apologize to you?

PETER. Oh for crying out loud.

ELLA. Peter what is the big deal?

PETER. The big deal is – oh FORGET IT.

> *(Angry now, he goes in to talk to MAUREEN. A pause between IAN and ELLA.)*

ELLA. I'm sorry about all this.

IAN. It's not really your fault.

ELLA. Well, last night.

IAN. We both behaved poorly last night.

ELLA. Well.

IAN. You know that's not why they're so upset, don't you?

ELLA. Everybody will feel better once we get some decent muffins.

IAN. I'm not entirely sure that will take care of it.

ELLA. Did you ever get your tea? I hope it's good. It should be good, I was guaranteed, you know, that it's the proper stuff. The tea bags are round, anyway. I always think that's a good sign.

> *(She sets it down, turns to get the milk. He reaches out and takes her hand. She looks at him, surprised that he has put his hand on her.)*

Ian.

IAN. Maureen told Peter that you and I were having an affair.

> *(a beat)*

ELLA. She told him what?

IAN. That you and I were sleeping together. She told him we were having an affair.

ELLA. Why did she tell him that?

IAN. Because I told her.

> *(They look at each other.)*

> *(The same moment. **ELLA** looks at **IAN**, shocked.)*

ELLA. You what?

IAN. I didn't mean to. She was being really provoking. And honestly I was tired of arguing with her. It gets wearing as I think you know.

ELLA. What did you tell her –

IAN. It's more like I let her think what she was thinking anyway. And then she told Peter. What she was thinking anyway. And now I rather think that he is thinking it too.

(He looks at her hand, massages it with his fingers. She yanks her hand back from him.)

ELLA. Hang on. You told Peter?

IAN. No, I didn't tell Peter anything.

ELLA. But you just said he thinks you and I –

IAN. I don't know what he thinks, I'm just guessing what he thinks.

ELLA. Wait, wait.

IAN. Sorry darling, you're just going to have to catch up.

(MAUREEN enters, PETER behind her. ELLA takes two quick steps away from IAN, managing to look terrifically guilty. MAUREEN stands there for a moment, looks back at PETER, looks back to IAN and ELLA.)

There you are. Feeling better?

MAUREEN. Yes.

(then)

I hope I'm not interrupting.

ELLA. Not at all.

MAUREEN. I was just thinking I'd get a cup of coffee.

IAN. Is there any?

MAUREEN. What are you drinking?

IAN. Ella just offered to make me a lovely cup of tea.

PETER. There's coffee, Maureen. Sit down, I'll get you a cup.

IAN. There's nothing to eat though. Those astonishing muffins are no longer with us. Tragically it seems Ella and I managed to do them in.

MAUREEN. You ate them all?

ELLA. We didn't actually. They just, they weren't very good so we threw them out.

MAUREEN. *(hostile)* They were very expensive.

ELLA. *(regrouping)* Oh I'm sure I just, I just I just, oh boy, I was going into town for some croissants. I'll pick up some juice and maybe some bagels and a paper, too, would anyone like a paper?

IAN. I'll come along, shall I?

ELLA. No!

IAN. I have some things I need to pick up at the chemist.

(ELLA *looks at him, startled, but he ignores her.*)

MAUREEN. You're going into town. You and Ella.

ELLA. No!

IAN. Yes, I was thinking I would.

PETER. Maybe we should all go. Go to brunch or something, that little bakery has a nice brunch.

IAN. You want to go to brunch?

PETER. Why not?

MAUREEN. Why not indeed?

ELLA. It's too early. It's early for brunch, isn't it?

PETER. We'll just call it food then.

ELLA. I'll just. I'll just. I can pick something up.

IAN. I still need to go to the chemist.

ELLA. No!

MAUREEN. I can't believe this.

IAN. Believe what?

PETER. There's that diner, we'll go to the diner.

IAN. Really? You like that diner?

MAUREEN. Well, I don't remember any diner.

IAN. Of course you do. The diner.

MAUREEN. Perhaps you went without me.

IAN. How would that be possible Maureen?

MAUREEN. I don't know. Maybe you went with Ella some time. How would I know.

ELLA. Why would I go to the diner with Ian?

IAN. I'm cut to the quick. Why wouldn't you is more the question, I would hope. Honestly. I'm a rather entertaining fellow I think in many ways! Last night's argument was an anomaly. Although I thought that was entertaining too, truth be told.

ELLA. The fact is I didn't go to the hideous and stupid and greasy diner with you, Ian –

MAUREEN. And yet he says he's been there.

ELLA. Well I don't know how he got there.

IAN. Really? You don't remember?

PETER. You know, I actually don't remember either. I mean, obviously I remember the diner. But I don't remember being there with you.

(*pause*)

IAN. Well I didn't actually say that you were there, Peter.

ELLA. Okay. Okay. We'll just, we'll just. We will all go to the diner.

IAN. That's ridiculous. Nobody likes that diner.

MAUREEN. There is no diner!

IAN. Of course there is. We all had lunch there two years ago. Really do not one of you remember this? It was the last time Maureen and I came up for one of these delightful weekends, we all had lunch there, and there ensued an endless discussion about which is greasier, American cuisine, so-called, or Irish cuisine, also so-called. I don't believe I was shouted down that time; I think I actually won that one. My position being that no one can outdo either me or my fellow countrymen when it comes to a dedication to lard.

(*There is a silence at this.*)

PETER. Oh that's right. We did, didn't we?

IAN. Yes.

PETER. Maureen, you remember –

MAUREEN. (*sharp*) No, I don't. Sorry. I don't.

PETER. It's that little place with the sort of horrible white siding, right across the street from the knitting place you like.

MAUREEN. I know the place you're talking about but I don't remember all of us having lunch there and arguing about lard!

PETER. No, we did. You had a salad I think. Something with tuna, you didn't like it. Well the food there is awful.

MAUREEN. I don't remember.

ELLA. Neither do I.

PETER. I do. The food there really is crap.

(*a pause*)

IAN. So what's the plan then? Crap food for four at the stupid hideous diner? Let's go.

(**IAN** *heads out the door, without looking back.*)

PETER. Come on Maureen.

(*He shows her out, they go. Finally* **ELLA** *follows.*)

End of Act One

ACT TWO

(Hours later. ELLA enters the kitchen, carrying a bag of groceries.)

ELLA. *(calling)* Peter don't yank up the basil please? I will handle it! I'm just getting a pair of scissors!

(IAN follows her in.)

IAN. You know the fact that you keep avoiding me is only making this worse.

ELLA. I'm not avoiding you. Christ I can't get away from you or your fucking wife.

(She sets down the groceries and looks for a scissors.)

IAN. You won't even look me in the eye. You look guilty as hell.

ELLA. I don't look guilty because I'm not guilty –

IAN. Aren't you?

ELLA. Jesus Ian this isn't funny. And now you've got Peter all tuned up.

IAN. He's doing that to himself.

(MAUREEN appears at the door, carrying groceries.)

MAUREEN. Could someone help me please?

IAN. Oh sorry.

(He opens the door, holds it for her. She hands him a bag.)

MAUREEN. There's more in the car.

IAN. I'll put these away while you fetch them.

(He smiles at her, easy, and starts to unload the groceries. She waits a moment, angry. ELLA steps in quick.)

ELLA. I'll get them.

>   *(She heads for the door.)*

IAN. But you're the only one who knows where everything goes.

ELLA. You're my guests; I can't have you running around like pack horses.

IAN. I can get them.

ELLA. Don't be ridiculous. Could you put the ice cream in the freezer though?

>   *(yelling)*

Peter, leave the basil, it needs to be cut!

>   *(And she goes. As soon as she's gone.)*

MAUREEN. You're ridiculous.

IAN. How so, my love?

MAUREEN. You're embarrassing yourself. Chasing after her like a dog in heat.

IAN. We had a deal, Maureen. When we talked, in the bedroom, before we all went out to that delicious lunch, you and I agreed there would be no more hysterics for the rest of the weekend. That was the deal, one day of self control. Our hosts have been begging us to leave but you wanted to stay –

MAUREEN. I wasn't the one who wanted to stay.

IAN. *(Overlap.)* You were embarrassed, you didn't want it getting back to Peter's brother that you humiliated yourself, you wanted a chance to behave better, that was what you wanted –

MAUREEN. I have been behaving. I have. While you, you flirt with her, you follow her around the grocery store like some sort of, like you're in heat –

IAN. I followed her around the grocery store like we were shopping for groceries!

MAUREEN. I said we should go. If you want to save our marriage, which I sincerely DOUBT, we need to go home now.

IAN. I am not doing this Maureen.

MAUREEN. Then that's fine you'll get nothing. I can prove psychological abuse, I can prove I can prove infidelity –

IAN. You can't prove anything.

MAUREEN. Psychological cruelty.

IAN. The public perception of our marriage is that you are a rampant nutcase and for years I have put up with your hysterics like a consummate gentleman.

MAUREEN. You married me for the money. Admit it.

IAN. Sorry, I thought it was the green card I was after –

MAUREEN. That's what mother said, from the start, you know he's only marrying you because of the money –

IAN. Your mother was a complete shrew, Maureen! She couldn't tolerate even the shred of a possibility that you might find happiness and so she poisoned the well from the start, we've been through this with eight separate therapists –

MAUREEN. This is not about my mother –

IAN. Then why do you keep bringing her up?

MAUREEN. Because she was right! She was right about you!

IAN. She was a hideous, jealous and frightened woman, and I regret sincerely the damage she did to your spirit and our marriage. Nevertheless. Nevertheless! I'm not interested in perpetuating this argument any further. You're right, we should divorce.

MAUREEN. What do you mean?

IAN. I mean I grant your request! I'm divorcing you. I want a divorce.

MAUREEN. This is what she said would happen.

IAN. Oh god.

MAUREEN. I want to go home.

IAN. We don't have a home any longer. That was your choice. You think I'm kidding I'm not kidding.

(**ELLA** *at the door, carrying bags, struggling with door…*)

ELLA. I think that's everything. I don't know what Peter thinks he's doing.

IAN. Here, let me –

> *(He goes to the door, opens it and takes bags from her.)*

ELLA. Thanks.

> *(**IAN** takes bags to the counter and starts to unload them as **ELLA** looks through some of the other bags.)*

Where are the scallops, did anyone get them into the refrigerator yet? I worry so about scallops, they seem dangerous don't they?

IAN. Actually they seem rather round and white and wobbly so no "dangerous" is not how I tend to see them, in my mind's eye.

ELLA. No I just mean you know shellfish. Like shellfish and refrigeration that seems like something you really need to pay attention to because if you don't something horrible might happen. Like dangerous like that. Maureen did you see them, did you already put them in the little meat bin?

MAUREEN. No actually I was too busy discussing our divorce with Ian. So I didn't actually put your fucking shellfish in the fucking meat bin.

> *(a pause)*

IAN. Besides which the meat bin would not be the proper place for shellfish. Here they are. I'll just put them on the middle shelf, shall I, looks like there's room there.

> *(He does. **ELLA** looks at them.)*

ELLA. Okay.

> *(**PETER** enters, carrying large basil plants, pulled out by their roots. He drops them on the counter.)*

PETER. Here's the basil.

> *(**ELLA** looks at it.)*

I got tired of waiting for the scissors.

ELLA. You killed my basil plant..

PETER. You asked for basil, I brought you the fucking basil.

ELLA. You – what – you – JESUS, Peter! You know how hard I, oh man, to figure out – how many years did, and then to actually get it to GROW. I can't, you KNOW the only thing I actually know how to cook is – and it took me six tries to get those fucking plants to grow out of the ground and this is the first year I've had an actual FUCKING CROP and it's ready it's Christ it's READY for me to actually do the, with the plastic containers and the harvest and the pine nuts and this is – fuck, I didn't even want a country home, that was your – I can't believe you did that. I can't believe you did that.

PETER. You kept telling me to wait for the scissors, and then you didn't bring the scissors! What was I supposed to wait out there all afternoon while you, while you –

ELLA. While I what. While I unloaded the car and listened to your friends explain that they are getting a divorce? Because that's what I've been doing. So that was a little distracting for a moment, but I certainly understand why you might have gotten impatient out there and consequently felt the need to murder my basil plants. I mean I do, I really understand that I just that is so mature. Really great. Really just fucking great.

> *(beat)*

IAN. Couldn't we run out now and buy some pine nuts and whip it all up in the blender right now?

ELLA. I'm not making pesto with you, Ian! Oh god. This is – I'm not kidding. I am not kidding.

> *(a long pause)*

PETER. You guys are getting a divorce?

IAN. No, look, it's not that big a deal. I mean, absolutely, I completely apologize for the way all this information, shall we say, is coming out. It was absolutely unintentional, god, of course we didn't come up here for the weekend thinking oh we're going to decide to split up anyway let's suck Peter and Ella into this in the most hideous way imaginable, obviously none of this was planned and it's ridiculous really that it would happen this way. I'm sure Maureen agrees with me that this is far from optimal, all of this, but all I mean is it's not – well, it's hardly a surprise, is it. To any of us. You've known, Peter, you told me before we were married that was unlikely to work out because Maureen was crazy.

(an awkward pause)

MAUREEN. You told him what?

PETER. I did not –

IAN. What does it matter. It was a long time ago.

PETER. I did not say that!

IAN. All I'm saying is no one possibly can be surprised. I'm not surprised. Maureen is certainly not surprised. And whatever you did or did not say nine or ten years ago, I can't believe you're surprised. Or Ella. You're not surprised, are you?

ELLA. I don't have an opinion.

MAUREEN. That's convenient.

ELLA. Convenient? I'm sorry, what did you say, "convenient?"

IAN. Would anyone like a glass of wine? Here's some of that good/bad Hungarian stuff. Maureen, would you like a glass? Peter?

PETER. Jesus. You actually expect us to have a drink and a chat about this?

IAN. Why not? You're two of our oldest friends, why not?

MAUREEN. Besides which, your wife – your wife –

ELLA. I what? What about me, Maureen? You're not going to repeat this ridiculous accusation that I've been, that Ian and I are having some sort of – god it's so insane I can't even say it! Is that what this is about? Is that why you're doing whatever you think you're doing? I mean, you can divorce him if you want I have no opinion on any of this BUT you cannot you cannot act like I have anything to do with it. Because that is nuts. You know that that is nuts. Right?

MAUREEN. Yes of course it's completely insane.

ELLA. Ian, would you tell her that she is mistaken about this – would you just tell her.

IAN. I would be happy to but I'm quite sure it wouldn't do any good. Maureen. This idea you've got, that I've somehow been untrue, it's nonsense. All right? Complete nonsense. I have been utterly faithful to you.

MAUREEN. Sure you have.

IAN. No really I have.

PETER. Maybe we shouldn't complicate things. Maybe you could just address the issue of whether or not you've been unfaithful with Ella.

(ELLA turns on him, edgy.)

ELLA. What is that supposed to mean?

PETER. It means it would be nice to clear this up.

ELLA. There is nothing to clear up!

PETER. Then he should have no problem saying it. Just to clear the air.

(There is a silence at this.)

IAN. Oh, sorry. My turn is it? What? What's needed? Another denial? I absolutely, without any hesitation whatsoever, completely and utterly deny that I have had any sexual intercourse with Ella. This weekend. Or any other weekend. Or weekdays either. Ever. How's that.

PETER. Fine. Thank you very much, Ian.

IAN. You're welcome, Peter.

(He gives ELLA a glass of wine. She doesn't look at him.)

MAUREEN. Well. Now that we've got that settled, and it's settled, apparently, that Ian and I are in fact divorcing, not because he and Ella did anything at all, because she's so innocent, innocent Ella, now that that is all straightened out, maybe Ian could return her earrings to her.

(a pause)

ELLA. What?

MAUREEN. Wouldn't you like them back?

ELLA. My earrings?

MAUREEN. They're in Ian's pocket. The right pocket. Of his pants.

ELLA. They are not.

MAUREEN. Silver? Dangly? Little red stones, those are yours, aren't they?

(beat)

PETER. Yes, I gave them to her for her birthday last year.

ELLA. Yes. Those, that is, I do have a pair of earrings like that. I mislaid them last night.

*(A pause. **IAN** pours wine. **ELLA** looks at him, looks at **PETER**.)*

I mislaid them!

PETER. Do you have Ella's earrings, Ian?

IAN. You know, actually I do, in fact. She's right, she mislaid them, and I picked them up. I meant to give them back this morning. I forgot I had them. Here.

*(He takes them out of his pocket, looks at them for a moment, then turns and gives them to **ELLA**.)*

ELLA. *(to **PETER**)* Listen. I don't know why he had my earrings.

PETER. It's fine, El.

ELLA. It isn't fine. It's anything but fine. Really. This is, you can't, Ian – tell him.

IAN. I meant to give them back. I just forgot.

ELLA. This is not my fault.

IAN. Absolutely not, it's no one's fault, no one at all.

*(**PETER** picks up the basil and **ELLA** goes to him.)*

ELLA. Peter –

>   (**PETER** *cocks his arms.*)

PETER. Don't touch me –

>   (*He drops the basil and goes.*)

ELLA. Peter –

>   (**ELLA** *follows* **PETER.**)

MAUREEN. Oh dear –

IAN. Yes –

>   (*then*)

Wine?

>   (*He hands her a glass wine. She takes a sip.* **IAN** *goes to the window and watches the action from there. As* **MAUREEN** *talks, he periodically goes to watch from the window.*)

MAUREEN. Well, I'm not surprised. At that little display.

IAN. You're not surprised that he tore up her basil plants? I am.

MAUREEN. Well, I knew him before any of you. In high school? He had a nasty temper. The kind of thing that would just snap, you know, god, he was famous! I've told you the stories. And now he's so smug about it. All these years, everyone, all the bragging at dinner parties. You'd get him a little drunk and hear about how he used to have a temper but he worked at it, it was something he was proud of, learning how to control that temper. I never bought it. I mean, I respected it, of course, of course you respect the attempt, but one time, I never told you this, it was just after college he was in the hospital for something – I can't remember what, appendicitis or gall bladder, something ridiculous, and I went in to say hello I hadn't seen him in years but I was trying to be nice, and he was still half, I don't know why they let me in, he was under the anaesthesia, still, to some degree, it was really, and he was positively hideous to me. I mean, I was just standing there with a little teddy bear, because you wanted to bring something, so I had this really cute, and he looked at me eyes half open, like a snake, or a crocodile – and he said – What the fuck do you think you're doing here? Seriously. No hello. No thanks for coming. Just what the fuck do you think you're doing here. And I thought, all that talk about how you've managed your temper. You haven't managed anything at all.

IAN. Did he bite you?

MAUREEN. What? No.

IAN. Did he strike you?

MAUREEN. No, I just said, he was half under the anaesthesia.

IAN. But you could see. That he hated you.

MAUREEN. He didn't hate me.

IAN. You just said he did.

MAUREEN. I didn't say that.

IAN. It didn't sound particularly friendly.

MAUREEN. He was anaesthetized.

IAN. So even when he was anaesthetized he disliked seeing you.

MAUREEN. No. That's not what I'm saying.

IAN. That seems to be what you're saying.

MAUREEN. What I'm saying is, he's hardly a saint.

IAN. I never thought he was.

MAUREEN. And he told you that I was crazy? He said that I'm the crazy one. I love that.

IAN. Well, it was a while ago, that he said it.

MAUREEN. But he said I was crazy.

IAN. He did, yes. At the engagement party, at Wendy what's her name's house, we were in the kitchen, looking for beers or something, and he said you know she's crazy. Talked a bit about how you used to date his brother and he thought you were just bonkers.

MAUREEN. I just love that.

IAN. Told me our marriage would be a disaster because of it, yes. A bit smug about it, actually.

MAUREEN. And then all these years he's like hello Maureen how are you?

IAN. Well, Maureen, what was he supposed to say? "How's that marriage going, you crazy woman, are both you and Ian as miserable as I predicted you would be?

MAUREEN. I always thought… I mean, don't laugh. But I, honestly, I always thought – he maybe had a little crush on me.

IAN. Did you?

MAUREEN. Don't sound so surprised, Ian lots of men find me attractive.

IAN. No, it's just, mere seconds ago you told a fascinating story, about seeing him in the hospital and he was a tad hostile –

MAUREEN. That was the anaeasthesia.

IAN. Ah.

MAUREEN. Besides that was a long time ago. I just mean, the past four or five years. He's always been so friendly. I really did think. Well, and I was right, wasn't I? They can act all superior, but maybe ours isn't the marriage that's in trouble after all.

>   (a beat)

IAN. Darling, you know, I wouldn't make a mistake about that.

MAUREEN. I just meant, compared to them.

IAN. Yes except… Just today, actually. You pointed out, you wanted a divorce, and I said yes I want that too. You remember this. It wasn't more than half an hour ago.

MAUREEN. People say things, Ian. You have to learn to forgive them.

IAN. Yes except Maureen darling you – well, really there's not much to say to that is there?

MAUREEN. No, because it's true.

IAN. No, it's because you really are just mad as a hatter.
And I say that with love, as much love as I have left after
all this time. I didn't see it at first because you know for
all those paranoid suspicions you hoard and nurture
you've quite forgotten the possibility that I was in love
with you. Honestly I thought you were exquisite, and
fun, darling, you really were, you were – well, what does
it matter. He was right; I was wrong; turns out you're
completely crackers. I'm not saying that I think you're
about to hole up in a clock tower somewhere and start
picking off undergraduates, one at a time or you know
I don't believe you're in psychic communication with
creatures from another galaxy. But you are just barking,
well what is insanity, you have to ask yourself. When so
many things, that vast unreason, or non reason at the
center of so much of what we face every day, we know
it's there, it plagues us, the thought that reality itself
truly might just be mad, the daily journey from dawn
to dusk carrying with it finally too many – too much –
Christ, god knows there's theories about all of it, whole
books about the workings of power and love and
science and history but they none of them ever I think
explain the essential – disappointment – of living with
so much insulting irrationality. Over time. So many
people appearing sane and then they say something or
do something, god, the sudden revelation of an interior
life that is completely well more than indefensible, how
many times are we supposed to accept the terror of
daily – and not only that. Or not even. Because the real
indignity, finally, is that crashingly horrifying discovery
that your soul was wrong. Was in fact just stupid, your
soul, and how do you live with that, how do you live
with the utter insult of cataclysmic personal mistakes?
Well we do. We just make do, god help us; we content
ourselves with the memory of a hope that it is possible,
perhaps to occasionally, at random, encounter a shred
of subjectivity that somehow lives in relation to your
shred, there's something else out there that for a
moment might recognize – you. The thing that is just

you, in your essence. Might be seen. By another shred. And the hope of that possibility calms you just enough to put up with the everyday madness and that helps you get used to it, doesn't it. Hope sustains us just enough actually, so that insanity – you know, the real thing, insanity – doesn't seem quite so dramatic. It's just the sea we swim in. It's just your wife. It's just you, darling. It's you.

MAUREEN. I have strong feelings, is that what you mean?

IAN. No. No, that's not actually what I mean.

> (**ELLA** *enters from the back door. She stares at them.*)

Are you all right?

ELLA. Yes. That is no, not all right – sorry, I'm really obviously Peter is terribly upset –

MAUREEN. I was just saying to Ian, and we think we have problems!

ELLA. No. No, there's no problems, it's just been difficult, and it's just this. I obviously, I have some cleaning up to do here! And Peter's upset. We both are – and and and he's driving back into the city for a little while, and you have to go. Now.

IAN. He went into the city?

ELLA. Yes, that's, he needs to cool off. And you have to go. I'm sorry.

MAUREEN. Of course you are.

ELLA. Oh boy.

MAUREEN. What? You apologize but you don't actually bother to pretend that you mean it. I mean, I can accept an apology but a fake apology, why should I?

ELLA. *(losing it now)* Yeah okay, I'm not sorry. I take it back. I take the apology back. Now can you just go! You guys both have made my life HELL for the past two days and now my marriage is in trouble and you can't be here when he gets back! You really, you have to GO.

MAUREEN. We've made the problem. I love that.

IAN. Well… Maureen…

MAUREEN. No. I don't accept that! This is all our fault? How can this be my fault? Peter is one of my oldest friends and I welcomed you. When he brought you to meet us, I was completely welcoming.

ELLA. Oh please. I can't do this –

MAUREEN. You can't, but you did. You made this happen.

IAN. Maureen darling?

ELLA. I didn't do anything except get into an argument with your fucking insufferable husband!

MAUREEN. Don't you dare talk about him that way.

ELLA. Can I talk about you that way?

IAN. I'm not actually sure that will prove to be the most useful tactic –

ELLA. So you have an useful idea? Ian! You actually are going to try to say something useful right now? Because I would like to hear that for once Ian I REALLY WOULD.

IAN. Maureen… We've been asked to leave.

ELLA. Thank you.

MAUREEN. I'm not going anywhere.

IAN. Yes in fact you are.

MAUREEN. None of our things are packed, Ian –

IAN. We'll get our things later. Come on.

MAUREEN. That's ridiculous. What are we supposed to do, just make another three hour drive, to come back up and get our things? Why should I be inconvenienced like that?

IAN. Get in the car.

MAUREEN. I will not be inconvenienced.

IAN. I mean it.

MAUREEN. I won't be silenced either. That's why you're so ready to leave all of a sudden, because you don't want to hear it anymore, well I will not be silenced!

IAN. Sorry, Ella. I am really sorry –

MAUREEN. I tell you I'm not leaving – Ian –

(For **IAN** *has taken her by the arm, and pushes her to the door.)*

IAN. Thanks, Ella, we had a terrific time, lovely, we'll do it again soon. Come on Maureen.

MAUREEN. *(overlap)* Stop it. Stop it! Let go of me – Ian – IAN.

(He opens the door and drags her outside. For a long moment, **ELLA** *is alone on stage. She waits. The sound of a car engine turning on, the car driving off. She looks around the kitchen, bereft. After a moment, she pours herself a glass of wine, drinks the whole thing. Shakes herself for a moment. Goes to the basil, starts to clean it up.)*

*(***IAN*** appears at the back door.)*

(She looks up.)

ELLA. Oh.

(She's tired, also a little relieved.)

What are you doing here? I heard the car go.

IAN. Maureen didn't want me.

ELLA. Well, you can't be here – I have to –

(She starts to cry. He goes to her. She cries on his shirt, then pushes him away.)

No. No. This is all your fault.

IAN. Look, I'm sorry about all of this, but did you honestly think they didn't know?

ELLA. They didn't because there was nothing to know.

IAN. They did because there was.

ELLA. We didn't do anything!

IAN. We did too. And they knew, maybe not literally, the specifics, but –

ELLA. Ian – I kissed you once, in a closet, a year ago. That's not the same thing as cheating. And for you to imply to anyone that it was more than that –

IAN. I didn't imply to anyone, I have honestly been silent as the grave but Ella, do me the decency to admit that it

was more than one kiss. We were in that closet for a full
fifteen minutes –

ELLA. Nothing happened!

IAN. Except that both of us have been thinking about it for
a whole year –

ELLA. I haven't.

IAN. Liar.

ELLA. I haven't been!

IAN. You avoid me. You can't stand it when I touch you.

ELLA. That's called being faithful, Ian!

IAN. But you're not faithful.

ELLA. Oh god I am too.

IAN. To a man who bores you.

ELLA. He doesn't!

IAN. Well he should because he is a colossal bore. Aside
from the excitement of watching him rip up your basil
plants there is really nothing to recommend the guy.
Plus he really is smug.

ELLA. He's fine!

IAN. Which is why you ended up in a closet with me.

ELLA. You really do, you have to go. He cannot find you
here.

IAN. You have a mistaken idea of morality.

ELLA. Hey, Ian! You don't get to define morality!

IAN. Listen, everyone assumes I'm some sort of insane
cheater because anyone in their right mind would
have cheated on Maureen but the fact is I was faithful.
Honestly, I was. I was trying to be good.

ELLA. Maybe you should keep trying.

IAN. Maybe I'm tired of it. You certainly are.

ELLA. I'm not!

IAN. Well I am, I really am. My father just died and I don't
want to lose my life. I don't want to lose it, Ella. I won't
lose anymore.

ELLA. I can't, I can't –

IAN. Can I tell you what he said about you? He said, you were full of light. He said that is a girl beyond time. He said, I see you look at her. Does she not see how you look at her? Well, he's gone. god help me I wish I could hear him one last time. I wish I could hear that Irish cadence again, I'm so tired of dreaming my past life, wishing toward the ghosts of what was, not even knowing if that was true when it was true! And the thing is, I meant, believed, that America could replace it, it's strength and beauty, the fierceness of the present isn't that what America is? The life we live now. god help me.

ELLA. I'm sorry, Ian – you know I am – but you, Maureen and you have to work this out. Somewhere else.

IAN. I tried. I did, I tried to leave a bunch of times and you wouldn't let me.

ELLA. That's not true.

IAN. It is absolutely true. You insisted I stay, Ella. You wanted me here, just as much as you wanted me in that coat closet.

ELLA. It wasn't a coat closet. It was a walk in closet!

IAN. It was a coat closet. And it was more than one kiss. And don't you dare even attempt to interfere with a memory virtually worn thin with everyday usage. I am here this weekend because of what happened in that coat closet and more to the point you invited me because of what happened in that coat closet. And you have seen me look at you. You live on it.

ELLA. That's not –

IAN. Don't. Don't try it. Because human beings are neither good nor evil, and your fantasy that remaining faithful to a broken marriage makes you a good person, frankly, is beneath you.

   (a beat)

ELLA. Okay. I will – concede – that there may be some logic in your allegation.

IAN. I don't accept your concession. I've been out here, throwing myself at your feet for two days. Do you really think I'm going to be satisfied with "I concede some logic –

ELLA. But my marriage is not broken.

IAN. All right, I'll consider rephrasing that bit. Your marriage is not happy.

ELLA. It is happy.

IAN. It is content.

ELLA. Yes.

IAN. It is not the soul-sapping disaster that my marriage to Maureen turned out to be, but Ella, it will not do.

ELLA. It does just fine! Peter is my best friend!

IAN. god, that sounds like death. Why do Americans persist in thinking that it is "moral" and "good" to remain addicted to an institution which has driven them mad? You all think the most insane and dangerous leaders imaginable are decent as long as they're in a supposedly sound marriage. The holiness of marriage is your security blanket, its the fog you wrap yourselves in so you can destroy yourselves without thinking about it. No, don't try to argue with me about this; that's not a debatable point. I'm from Ireland; self destruction is something we understand. And besides, let me tell you, everyone on the planet is talking about it. We're crushed, honestly. Do you think we weren't rooting for you? Because we were. You were our dream. And then you threw it away, you threw away the Enlightenment, for what? For marriage? I'm telling you, the entire planet is crushed.

ELLA. What are we talking about now? Marriage, politics, global history –

IAN. We're talking about goodness, your favorite subject. Because it all comes back to that, darling. Why on earth are you trying so hard to be good, if goodness is death? Or not even that. What is it's just an anaesthetic? If goodness is just an anaesthetic is it still goodness?

Especially if anaesthesia isn't finally just an excuse to release the worst in us. Our own little excuse for poor behavior.

(a beat)

ELLA. You know honestly Ian, I can't tell if this is a seduction, or a lecture.

IAN. Oh! Sorry. I did drift, didn't I? Here, let me clear that up for you.

(He goes to kiss her.)

ELLA. Wait.

(then)

IAN. No more waiting Ella. You know I'm right. You recognize me. We share a shred of subjectivity. And I will not lie about that, and I will not live without that anymore. Aww come on, they both think we've already slept together anyway. It has a certain sublime logic, you must admit. And it adds a delightful dimension to the questions surrounding the morality of all this. If your spouses know, or think they know, that you've already done it, is it immoral to then follow through? It's like that tree falling in the wood, you kind of have to think about it.

(a beat)

Ella. The Gods have given you a great gift. If you are granted a reprieve, a real reprieve from how you choose to live, how will you behave?

ELLA. Oh the gods gave me that.

(ELLA turns away.)

IAN. You're tempted. You are. You've been thinking about it. Admit it. You've been thinking about having sex with me.

ELLA. Thinking is not the same thing as doing it. It isn't a sin.

IAN. It is actually; it's one of the top ten. If you'd like, I'd be happy to introduce you to one or two of the others.

ELLA. *(laughs)*

IAN. We just got through sin number three, darling, catch up. We're on to number six.

> *(He kisses her. They start to seriously make out. Clothes are coming off. He grabs her by her shirt and drags her off, to the downstairs bedroom. Lights shift.)*

> *(It is the middle of the night. The kitchen is empty. Off stage, the sounds of laughter and sex. Then silence. Then more laughter, and then some more sex. Whatever is going on is tender and beautiful.)*

> *(***ELLA*** *enters, goes to the refrigerator. She wears underwear and something loose on top, which she pulls on as she moves.)*

ELLA. Are you hungry?

IAN. Starving.

> *(***IAN*** *enters behind her.)*

ELLA. There's lots of, we ended up with so much food...

IAN. Just don't offer me muffins.

ELLA. I can't see anything. I hate this house. You know how some places, when it's dark, you still know where you are? I can't see anything in the dark here. It's not intuitive.

IAN. Don't turn on the light.

> *(He kisses her.)*

ELLA. And you know what else? I hated those basil plants. I'm so glad he tore them up. Where are those scallops?

IAN. Scallops? There's something peculiarly perverse – scallops?

ELLA. We could fry them up...

IAN. That will take too long.

(He grabs her and starts to kiss her again. They start to make out by the refrigerator. They are really into it. IAN picks up ELLA, sits her on the counter. The door of the refrigerator swings open, and the light reveals PETER, sitting across the room, on the floor, watching. They don't see him for a moment.)

ELLA. You know what?

IAN. What?

ELLA. Making out with you in that closet was fun, but this is better.

IAN. It is.

(She giggles as they continue to make out.)

PETER. Did you tell your wife, "I wish you were dead?"

(IAN and ELLA freeze.)

ELLA. Shit. Peter?

(She tries to get off the counter, but IAN holds her there. He turns.)

IAN. Hello, Peter. Didn't expect to see you back this evening. Ella said you'd gone back to the city.

(PETER stands, turns on a light.)

PETER. Answer the question. Did you say, to Maureen, "I wish you were dead."

IAN. Is that really what's worrying you right now, Peter?

PETER. I want her to know.

ELLA. Peter – this is, this should not, you can't –

PETER. Tell her! Tell her that you said it!

IAN. It's not outside the realm of possibility. She is a rather provoking personality as I believe you know.

PETER. He said, "I wish you were dead," to a woman who is known to be suicidal –

IAN. What she is, actually, is "operatic."

PETER. You want to know what happened? You want to know where she is now?

IAN. Not particularly. But if you have any curiosity about Ella, and her activities, you should CHECK IN WITH ME.

ELLA. Hey! Knock it off.

PETER. Do you think you could be decent enough to put some clothes on, or is that sort of thing beneath you now?

> *(She goes up the stairs to her bedroom.* **IAN** *and* **PETER** *consider each other.)*

Enjoying the weekend?

IAN. Very much so. How about you?

PETER. I've had better. These country houses sometimes you just have to admit that they're really kind of a disappointment. You sink a lot of money into them just for the chance to get away and forget your life, that's their point isn't it? Some place you can go to keep everything else at bay. An island castle. Peace. Tranquility. Someone breaches the ramparts, it actually kind of pisses you off.

> *(He picks up the frying pan, considers it.)*

IAN. If the point is tranquility, you might consider moving to the moon.

PETER. You don't get to offer advice, shithead.

> *(He suddenly swings the frying pan at* **IAN,** *who ducks and goes down.* **PETER** *is coming after him with the frying pan. He shoves a chair out, which impedes* **PETER** *but doesn't bring him down.)*

IAN. Peter, Peter I can have you arrested for this! This ISN'T a medieval fortress you know, you're not actually allowed to strike people at your own whim because you've been provoked. No one is going to see your side of things, and you will end up in jail!

PETER. You know what? You talk too much.

> *(***PETER** *brings down the frying pan,* **IAN** *rolls away and barely misses getting brained a second*

time. **ELLA** *appears at the doorway, wearing jeans and a sweater. She leaps on* **PETER**.)

ELLA. STOP IT. STOP IT.

(She takes the frying pan from **PETER**'*s hand and throws it in the sink.* **PETER** *looks around, finds a bottle of wine and a glass, starts to drink.)*

PETER. Maureen, in case you're wondering – Maureen is in the hospital.

She started to drive back to the city. Next thing she knows she's being pulled over. Apparently she was clocking more than a hundred miles an hour. And she'd been drinking. And she's in hysterics. So they ARREST her. And then she calls me. Well, she can't call her husband, can she, so she calls me, to come bail her out. By the time I get there, she's been in a holding cell, crying and screaming for three hours straight, and they're putting her in an AMBULANCE to take her to the HOSPITAL where she is now sedated and under observation because they've got her on SUICIDE WATCH. Anything else you need to know?

IAN. No that would cover it.

PETER. And you don't even care! Look at him – he doesn't even react!

IAN. You seem to be doing enough reacting for both of us, I thought I'd take the night off.

PETER. Yeah, that's clever. Hilarious. Dazzling. Is that what you want, El? Really? That's what you want now, just a clever – liar –

ELLA. I am not talking about this, like this. I am not doing this.

PETER. He's just a liar, he's a trickster, he destroys things, look at this, he's destroyed three lives, without even, he's a destroyer and you are letting him, why, why –

ELLA. You believed it before it happened! You opened the door.

PETER. And you just walked through it.

IAN. We all did. Including you. What hospital is she at.

> *(a beat)*

What hospital?

PETER. Columbia Methodist.

IAN. All right if I use your phone? Thanks.

> *(He takes the phone and goes off.* **PETER** *and* **ELLA***, for a moment, alone.)*

PETER. Get your things.

ELLA. *(stunned)* What?

PETER. We won't talk about it. We'll talk about it later.

ELLA. I can't go home with you – now – Peter –

PETER. Why? Because of this? This is nothing! This is a game to him! You heard him admit it!

ELLA. That's not why.

PETER. I told Maureen she was nuts. I told her I didn't believe it. All these years, I tried to deny it –

ELLA. All these years it wasn't happening!

> *(beat)*

But it is happening now.

> *(There is silence at this.)*

> *(***IAN*** enters, dressed. He holds up the phone, puts it back in its cradle.)*

IAN. Thanks.

PETER. You talked to the hospital?

IAN. Yes. She's happily sedated. Doing fine. Under observation. Under control.

PETER. Are you going over there?

IAN. Are you offering me a ride?

> *(A beat.* **PETER** *shifts, looks at* **ELLA***.)*

PETER. I thought you were perfect. Not perfect, but perfect for me. I thought you were good in a way that wasn't nothing. I felt that we were good together. And that was enough, it was reason enough to wake up in

the morning. And to do the things that make up a life.
I don't know why we're here. I don't know what we owe
to the world. But to me, you were good.

(beat)

I'll call you tomorrow. Okay?

(She doesn't respond. He goes. After a moment,
there is the sound of a car door, and then a car
driving off.)

ELLA. You want some tea?

IAN. Tea. Brilliant.

(She starts to make tea.)

ELLA. How are you getting to the hospital?

IAN. Oh, I hadn't thought about that.

ELLA. You can call a taxi. It's a ways but they'll come out
here.

IAN. Oh good.

(beat)

Then you're just going to stay. Here.

ELLA. I don't know. Peter is probably going to bug the shit
out of me, to get me to come home. Eventually he'll
come up and insist. Probably bring me a present.

IAN. Will it be a nice present?

ELLA. I don't know. I really don't know.

(beat)

You want milk?

IAN. No, actually, I don't want milk. I mean, really, Ella.
What are you on about?

ELLA. What?

IAN. Honestly, this is so dreary. This is the most dreary I've
ever seen you.

ELLA. You didn't find that – interruption – upsetting?

IAN. Well, it was regrettable.

ELLA. Regrettable?

IAN. Yes because we were having a nice time and now we're having tea.

ELLA. Sorry. Unlike you I seem to need a moment to regroup. Watching my marriage go up in flames was a little disconcerting.

IAN. But you were bored in that marriage.

ELLA. I am sorry to have hurt my husband!

IAN. He tried to brain me with a frying pan!

ELLA. It's not like he wasn't provoked.

IAN. I didn't provoke him! He suspected all along! He just told you, he suspected all along!

ELLA. Yes he did tell me that.

> *(beat)*

He told me that while you were in the other room on the phone with the hospital.

IAN. I was not in the other room on the phone with the hospital, please. I was eavesdropping, behind the door.

ELLA. You didn't call the hospital?

IAN. Listen, Maureen is fine at that hospital. She will have a lovely night's sleep, and the doctors will be much nicer to her than I would. She's fine.

ELLA. So what are we supposed to do now?

IAN. I expect nothing but I have reason to hope. Before we were interrupted I was ready to go the rest of the weekend, and call in sick on Monday, maybe call in sick on Tuesday too. I see no reason to alter the plan.

ELLA. Ian, did you do this?

IAN. What?

ELLA. All of this. Did you make it happen? Did you deliberately – destroy our lives? For this?

IAN. Would that be a good thing, or a bad thing?

> *(She considers this. They consider each other. Blackout.)*

End of Play